For Maurice Gilmour – C.M.

Text copyright © 2004 by Colin McNaughton. Illustrations copyright © 2004 by Satoshi Kitamura.
The rights of Colin McNaughton and Satoshi Kitamura to be identified as the author and illustrator of this work
have been asserted by them in accordance with the Copyright, Designs and Patents Act, 1988.
First published in Great Britain in 2004 by Andersen Press Ltd., 20 Vauxhall Bridge Road, London SW1V 2SA.
Published in Australia by Random House Australia Pty., 20 Alfred Street, Milsons Point, Sydney, NSW 2061.
All rights reserved. Colour separated in Italy by Fotoriproduzioni Grafiche, Verona.
Printed and bound in Italy by Grafiche AZ, Verona.

10   9   8   7   6   5   4   3   2

British Library Cataloguing in Publication Data available.

ISBN 1 84270 309 9

This book has been printed on acid-free paper

Once Upon An Ordinary School Day

Story by Colin McNaughton
Pictures by Satoshi Kitamura

AndersenPress
London

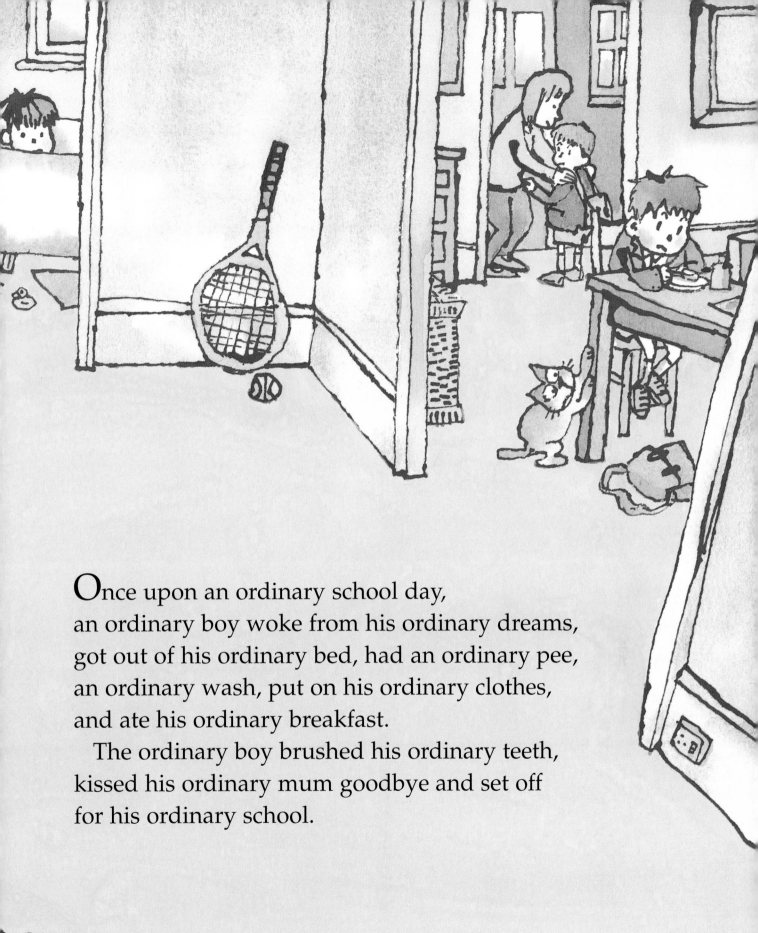

Once upon an ordinary school day,
an ordinary boy woke from his ordinary dreams,
got out of his ordinary bed, had an ordinary pee,
an ordinary wash, put on his ordinary clothes,
and ate his ordinary breakfast.
   The ordinary boy brushed his ordinary teeth,
kissed his ordinary mum goodbye and set off
for his ordinary school.

And as he walked through the ordinary streets,
past the ordinary shops and across the ordinary roads,

the ordinary boy thought his ordinary thoughts.

And when he reached the ordinary school the ordinary boy had an ordinary game of football with his ordinary friends until the ordinary school bell rang.

The ordinary boy went into his ordinary
classroom and sat at his ordinary desk.
Then, something quite out of the
ordinary happened . . .

"Good morning, everybody!"
said a quite extraordinary figure
bounding into the classroom.
"My name is Mister Gee
and I'm your new teacher.
Now, you don't know me and
I don't know you,
so, to help me *get* to know you,
I've had an idea . . ."

As Mister Gee handed out paper
he said, "For our first lesson together
I want you to listen to some music and
I want you to let the music make
pictures in your heads.
Is that clear?"

And the ordinary children whispered: "He's barmy!"
"He's bonkers!" "He's as nutty as a fruitcake!" "Music?"
"Pictures?" "What's he on about?" And Mister Gee said,
"Shush, just close your eyes, open your ears and listen."

And the music began:
a rumbling, rolling,
thunderous music
that boomed and
crashed around
the classroom.

Suddenly it stopped. And Mister Gee said:
"Tell me what the music made you think of."
One girl shouted, "Stampeding horses!"
Someone else said, "No, it was racing cars!"
And the ordinary boy said, "I saw elephants, Sir,
and there were hundreds of them!"

"Yes," laughed Mister Gee. "Isn't it wonderful?
Now, I want all of you to try to put
what you hear on paper.
Start writing!"

And as the music
grew and swooped and
danced and dived once more,
the ordinary boy began to write.
He used words he didn't fully understand
and his story made no sense but it didn't matter
and he didn't care. And he wrote as fast as he could
but it would never be fast enough – there was just too
much to say. It was as if a dam had burst in his head
and words just came flooding out . . .

. . . and the words were his toys and he was lost,
lost in the game – the story-telling game.
      And it was *extraordinary* . . .

And the other children?
Some wrote stories about giants
and some about magic. Some wrote of brave girls
and some of boys with lightning-shaped scars
on their foreheads.
    Some just made stuff up because
the music didn't mean anything to them
and Pauline Crawford read *The Beano*.

Some wrote stories
they thought would please
the teacher and some became
heroes and some became villains
and some thought the whole thing
was silly and Billy Pearson fell asleep –
"Perchance to dream,"
said Mister Gee.

And at the end of that extraordinary school day,
the ordinary boy saw Mister Gee getting into his car.
"Sir," said the ordinary boy, "that was the best lesson ever.
I've never felt like that before. It was magic!"
"Still think I'm bonkers?" said Mister Gee, smiling.
The ordinary boy blushed.
"I can't wait to read your story tonight,"
said Mister Gee. "See you tomorrow."
And he disappeared in a cloud of smoke
out of the school gates.

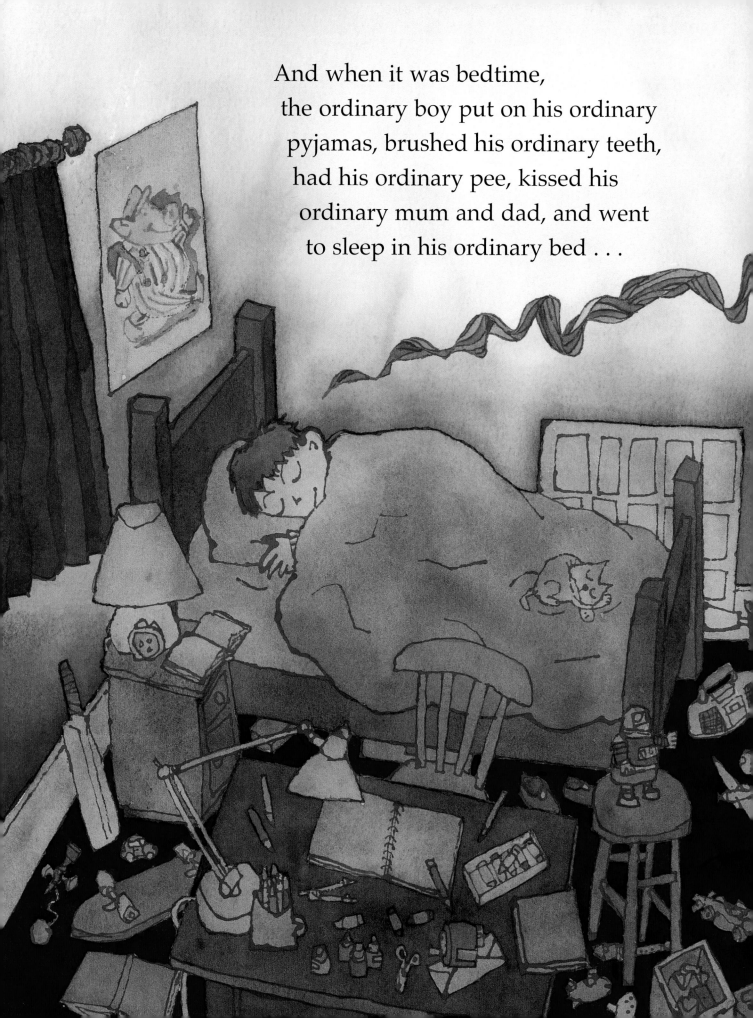

And when it was bedtime,
the ordinary boy put on his ordinary
pyjamas, brushed his ordinary teeth,
had his ordinary pee, kissed his
ordinary mum and dad, and went
to sleep in his ordinary bed . . .

. . . and had
extraordinary
dreams.